The Strange Tale of Billy McGinty

Wiley Traylor

Published by Wiley Traylor, 2022.

This is a work of fiction. Similarities to real people, places, or events are entirely coincidental.

THE STRANGE TALE OF BILLY MCGINTY

First edition. June 23, 2022.

Copyright © 2022 Wiley Traylor.

ISBN: 979-8201303358

Written by Wiley Traylor.

Table of Contents

Note to the Reader

The character that is telling this story is a young Scottish lad. A proper treatment would be to present the dialog in the Scottish language; however, the author is not Scottish, nor does he wish to offend the Scottish by misapplying what he would think to be Scottish words or mannerisms. In order to present the story in a format that is readable to others of the English language, only small portions of the Scottish language (the occasional aye, wee, laddie, or ye) are employed in the quoted conversations of the characters, and only then to add a subtle reminder to the reader that the characters are indeed Scottish. The author means no disrespect to any of Scottish heritage.

Cover photo from pixabay/adrianseedhill

The Encounter

I would like to recount to you a story told to me quite a few years ago by a young lad I met at a train station west of London while sitting out a particularly heavy downpour of the most bone-chilling rain. I had retired to a small tea room in the station for coffee when the rain-soaked lad slipped quietly in and took a seat near the front window. I could see he was cold as evidenced by the trembling of the edge of his much worn jacket, so feeling some measure of compassion, I brought him a cup of hot tea and a scone and sat down across the table from him.

He thanked me of course, and after some minor chatter between strangers about the rain, the delayed train schedule and other non-descript conversation, he suddenly grew very quiet and asked me if I'd like to hear a story. Thinking it would be but a simple story, I thought nothing contrary and agreed to hear his tale, and settled back in my chair. He sat quietly for a brief moment, his eyes staring out the window as if what he was about to say was somehow written on some unseen manuscript, and that the story was of such importance that it needed to be well understood.

He began slowly by saying that he was from western Scotland and that he was making his way back home after having spent some time in the south of England with some distant relatives.

He took a sip of tea, cleared his throat, and started gently.

"Should you ever find yourself driving up the northwest coast of Scotland, about two miles south of Scourie, just past the old Macdonough croft, you may see a place in the wall on the eastern side of the road where the stonework looks a little different. Not so easily noticed by the casual passerby, but a closer look will reveal a slightly different pattern and age to the stones that make up that portion of the wall. It is all that is left of any evidence of a gate that once led to a homestead that belonged to my great-great grandfather of many years ago.

After his premature death in the hills where he herded his sheep, brought on by the impact of an overly enthusiastic charge of one of his Border Collies that knocked him off balance and sent him tumbling down the jagged edges of the rocks to the ground below, my great-great grandmother, who had married quite young, remained there as best she could, crofting only as much as she needed for food and hay for the small number of animals she kept.

It was a very simple home, built in the day when function and protection from the weather were its primary designs. The first room encountered when coming in from the elements consisted mainly of the hearth, an imposing structure that provided sufficient comfort for even the harshest of winter days. Above it sat a simple wooden timber that traversed the entire width of the design, deeply imbedded into the stone upon which rested the treasures of the house: an old but still magnificent clock that chimed the hours faithfully, two old oil lanterns that provided the light for the windowless room, a humidor of the finest tobacco available to them, and a collection of pipes that had not been used since the day of my great-great grandfather's death.

Off to one end of the room was the single bedroom and through a broad door just to the left of the hearth and directly behind the large hearth lay the kitchen that now held a large cast iron stove that my great-great grandmother had purchased shortly after she sold the majority of her flock that she had come to despise following her husband's untimely death."

A Point in History

He took a bite of scone and another sip of tea and continued.

"It was here one stormy night in late 1944 that World War II became very personal to my great-great grandmother in the form of loud pounding at her door. She had always hoped that any such disturbance at such a wicked hour of the night might be one or both of her sons who had been for some many months now locked in service to the King on some distant unknown battlefield.

But upon arousing and lighting one of the old lanterns, and grabbing the old shotgun she kept handy for such unwanted intrusions, she opened the door and found to her dismay three German sailors, wounded and soaked from the late autumnal storm that had blown in earlier that evening and was at that very moment, with great gusts of wind, blowing rain over the heads of the three shadowy figures and into her house.

Being a widow now these several years, she had always kept the old shotgun loaded, which she immediately raised and pointed directly at the three men, now seriously surprised by such an unexpected response. The one in the middle spoke softly and with great raspy effort, but in surprisingly understandable English, explaining that their intentions did not warrant the two large barrels of the 12 bore now not three feet from his face.

He was obviously the more seriously wounded of the three, as evidenced by the tremendous effort put forth by the men who flanked him who struggled to keep him and themselves upright against the force of the wind which pressed them forward with each gust.

In labored breathing, he asked if they might find shelter from the storm, for they had only that night escaped the sinking of their U-boat and had been blown ashore by the cold winds of the Atlantic.

Upon demanding they surrender their arms to her, which consisted of only two water soaked pistols, and only upon their acknowledgement that they were from that moment on now her prisoners, did my great-great grandmother agree to allow them entry into her home, for she felt no inclination to assist these whose armies elsewhere were tearing her world apart.

But alas, her sense of Christian charity overrode her initial sense of hatred and after allowing them to take their rest near the dying coals of the fireplace, she slipped quietly into the kitchen and opened the rear door only far enough to toss the pistols into the rain-soaked darkness.

Then searching her small larder for some bread and brandy, she retrieved a small loaf and a half-empty bottle she kept for medicinal purposes, which she extended in their direction and they accepted, with gratitude.

Convinced that she would not be attacked, she withdrew to the bedroom, removed the coverings from her own bed and presented them to the men who had just stoked the fire with a few pieces of driftwood and peat from the box near the hearth and were at that moment rubbing their stiff and slightly purple hands together in anticipation of the soon to be had warmth.

She then moved quietly into her sparse kitchen and with the addition of several pieces of peat into the stove, began the process of making tea. While the kettle was coming to a boil, she examined the wounded man and to her great relief found that his injury was not life threatening and in fact was a large piece of a shell fragment imbedded quite deeply in the back of his left thigh.

To her further relief, though its ragged edges lay dangerously close to the main artery, it had severed neither artery nor large vein. Pouring a small trickle of brandy on the wound and with the expertise of someone who had on occasion stitched up an injured calf, she removed the fragment, closed the wound, and wrapped it with raggedy ribbons of cloth torn from one of her late husband's old shirts.

The noise from the kitchen reminded her that the peat fire had done its work and she slipped away quietly to make a very large pot of tea. The history of tea in Scotland is the subject for another time but suffice it to say, that of all the liquids consumed in that area, perhaps none has the varied repertoire of benefits as does tea. Be it depression, illness, injury, broken relationships, chill, contemplative thought, or the cruelty and rigors of war, nothing can compare to its restorative powers or its ability to remove barriers between strangers.

Therefore, it should not be surprising that the tea, combined with yet another morsel of bread with butter and honey should open the lips of her new prisoners of war.

In a few minutes, revived somewhat by the sparse offerings, and warmed by the fire, the captain, having spotted the collection of pipes and the humidor, politely inquired if he might have a pipe, to which my grandmother reluctantly agreed. She surveyed the collection, and selecting the one pipe that her late husband rarely used, presented it and the humidor to the captain who accepted it with gratitude."

The Battle Plan

After two or three quick bites of the scone, the lad, now warmed somewhat by the tea, resumed his story.

"Not long after he had taken a few deep draws from the pipe, the captain, now fully at peace with his captor, began to speak.

Though he told her only a little about who they were in their days before the war in their peaceful life east of Berlin, it surprised her that he would divulge, in some unexpected detail, the circumstances that had led the three of them to her door.

For only the morning before, the captain had determined it was his time to go all out in the war against the shipment of arms in the North Atlantic, and had decided that he would station himself as close as possible to the movement of ships in and out of Loch Ewe. For there he was certain that he could fire all of his complement of torpedoes into a sea of departing ships and amass the quantity of sunken tonnage that he needed to achieve the coveted promotion he had sought since 1939. For though he had circumnavigated the British Isles and spent considerable time in the North Atlantic, he had but only one victory to his credit, a small American freighter of only some 7000 tonnes.

But alas, as was later revealed to my great-great grandmother by neighbors whose predisposition in life was to hear all and tell all, unbeknownst to him at the time and in his excitement of the moment, the captain and his second in command had failed to notice a small lad on one of the outer islands flying a kite in the stiff breeze that often precedes one of the approaching storms of that area.

The bespectacled lad, whose glasses had not been cleaned in some many days, upon seeing the periscope and thinking he had seen the much-sought-after Loch Ness monster, excitedly told a local policeman. The policeman, despite much effort, could not convince the lad of the improbability of the monster being so far from his home in Loch Ness, suddenly realized the dangers of what the lad had seen and in turn notified the Royal Navy detachment at Loch Ewe.

Upon stationing his U-boat at what he thought to be his most advantageous point, the captain remained submerged throughout the day, occasionally elevating and peering through his periscope as he tracked and recorded in his log the ships that navigated the waters in and around the loch. It was a risky move, but thinking the Royal Navy would never expect a German U-boat captain to be so bold, and trying to minimize usage of his batteries, he remained relatively stationary throughout the day. His plan was to strike when darkness fell, sink his desired quota, and retreat to the open waters of the North Atlantic in a high-speed surface escape.

The U-boat captain had throughout the daylight hours elected to use some clever power saving techniques to keep his boat "pointed" toward the open sea, with the aft facing the small island as closely as he dared. Natural ocean currents would gradually slip the ship and necessitate the use of his electric motors from time to time throughout the day to keep his boat on position.

Also, unbeknownst to him at the time (as later revealed yet again by certain acquaintances of my great-great grandmother), the commander of the Royal Navy, upon hearing of the sighting of the young lad, had dispatched to the area a destroyer and a corvette that remained out of sight to the north around the bend of the island until another corvette could be dispatched from the opposite direction, thus hemming the U-boat between them.

During these brief periods of movements, SONAR operators on the corvettes were able to determine his exact position and consequently when the Navy attack commenced, the corvettes, equipped with the latest Hedgehog technology, destroyed the U-boat quite quickly with a minimum of ordinance. Why they waited until near sundown to attack was never explained, but the outcome cannot be disputed.

One side of the boat's hull was split open, and in an attempt to surface so his crew could abandon ship, the captain was able to point the bow of the boat upward only long enough that the crew could deploy the life rafts and escape the boat which then sank quite quickly. The accuracy of the naval gunners was of such effectiveness that several 5-inch shells struck the U-boat tower where the captain had taken his stand to go down with his boat. The blast hurled him violently overboard where two of his crew fetched his wounded body from the sea, and in the cover of darkness, somehow paddled out of sight of the corvettes whose lights now scanned the surface of the water. Convinced that the captain had gone down with the ship, and aware of the storm now beginning to show its might, the corvettes soon left the area with what enemy crew they could fetch from the cold waters.

Aided by the winds of the storm that soon became quite strong, the two crew members made their way to shore in the darkness with their wounded captain, and after struggling with the large slippery rocks at the water's edge, crossed the road and made their way up the gentle slope to the house where they now rested before a warm fire."

The Arrest

I started to interrupt the lad to ask if the story would be much longer, but a certain curiosity began to build in me causing me to hold my question, and he continued.

"Though only the captain spoke English, my great-great grandmother was quite certain the other two seemed to be well aware of the details their captain had shared and thus all three appeared to wait in anticipation of how she would respond.

'Do I need to be fearing for my life?' she asked as she searched her memory for where she had placed the old shotgun.

'Nein,' the captain declared solemnly with a tone of exhaustion and resolve, for it had been a very long and weary war, and now seeing up close and personal the determination and ability of the Allies to obtain a full and total victory, he himself had resolved that his fight was now over. To escape the safety of the house and the warmth of the fire for a chance of traveling across the breadth of all of northern Scotland to yet another span of impassable water was in his mind a most futile exercise.

His devotion to his crew was such that he thought it a most unwise idea to subject them to any further danger, for they had served him well these five long, arduous years and to present them the possibility of death at the hands of some angry crofter did not now seem so noble and would likely serve neither the Führer nor the fatherland. So with that resolve, he awaited his fate at the hands of this seemingly gentle woman.

He had not long to wait, for in those hours before sunrise, the ordeal, the warm fire, and the brandy had taken their toll and he and his companions slipped effortlessly into sleep. As is common for all who close their eyes in rest, the night passes in but an instant.

Shortly after sunrise, there came again a knock at the door, which upon opening revealed a young lieutenant and several soldiers with arms at the ready. For in their haste to escape the frigid clutches of an angry sea, the three sailors had neglected to hide their raft, and naval patrols who had resumed their search for any possible additional survivors, and those who often harvest the bounty of flotsam given up by the sea, had reported the location of the raft. Even the dimmest of dimwits could not have overlooked the croft that lay across the road and directly up the hill from where the three had emerged from the sea.

Upon seeing that the three posed no threat to his men, the lieutenant entered quietly, and after reassuring himself that the woman of the house had not been harmed, several of his men immediately escorted the three weary sailors from the house into an awaiting truck.

As he prepared to leave, he hesitated, looked past the old woman, and then searched the kitchen and then the bedroom, and after convincing himself there were no others to be found, he addressed the woman.

'You know, it could be said by some that you were in fact aiding and abetting the enemy.'

'Nonsense young man,' she said abruptly and sternly. 'They were my prisoners, captured at gunpoint, and ordered to surrender their arms. In fact, if ye will look out back, somewhere in the mud ye will find two pistols.'

Upon hearing that, the lieutenant spoke to one of his men who after a few minutes returned with two German pistols somewhat covered in muck.

'Very well,' the lieutenant replied, now convinced that this woman had not been harboring enemy combatants. 'Is there anything I can do for you before I leave?'

'Aye,' she said authoritatively, 'I'd like a receipt for my prisoners.'

'Pardon?' he asked, obviously caught off guard by the strange nature of her request.

'Aye, a receipt for three prisoners of war. You know, names, ranks, and serial numbers. Surely ye must have some kind of documentation that you military folk process when prisoners are transferred.'

Still somewhat taken aback, the lieutenant sent one of his men out to the truck to secure from the attending sergeant the information she wanted that he then presented to her.

'A grateful nation salutes you. Will there be anything else?' he asked somewhat sarcastically.

'Aye, as matter of fact, you could replace my bit of brandy,' she said, pointing to the empty bottle on the hearth.

'I'll see what I can do,' he said sheepishly as he bid her farewell, slipped quietly out the door, into the truck and sped away.

My great-great grandmother then closed the door on this intrusion into her somewhat unremarkable life and retired to her bedroom for a bit of rest before commencing her day's chores, which now included the additional task of airing her bedcovers that reeked of the sea and of men who had not washed in a while."

The Story Continues

"That is quite some story, young man," I told him as he took several bites and finished the scone.

"But there's more," he replied as he took the last sip of tea and slid the empty cup in my direction. Still feeling compassion for him, I sought out another cup of tea and returned to the table. He continued.

"Had it not been for the pipe that unexpectedly departed with the captain, the story would end here. For though it was a memorable ordeal for my great-great grandmother, in the overall grand scheme of things of war, it was indeed only one insignificant night with no apparent consequences.

For her, life continued as before, one difficult day drifting into another that made up the tedious weeks that comprised the grueling months that then carried over into yet another year. And in the new year, 1945 brought the inevitable end to the hopes of the 3rd Reich and with it, the return of one of her two sons, whose safe return was celebrated by her neighbors and friends along with numerous, somewhat fictional, accounts of how his mother had singlehandedly captured an entire submarine crew. Her second son, of whom some thought had been a casualty of war, later sent word that he had survived the war and had remained on active duty as part of the occupation forces stationed in post-war Germany.

However, for the German POWs held in England, life did not return to normal. Many continued to be held prisoner for many months, even years, following the cessation of hostilities. Some were held to help rebuild the cities and streets their bombs had destroyed and some, through certain freedoms granted them while POWs, had met and fallen in love with British women and consequently sought citizenship in England.

For others the news was bad. Such was the case of this captain who, through somewhat confused official channels, had learned that he had lost his wife and daughter and his home that had been reduced to rubble was now in Soviet-held territory. These sorrowful few felt they had no other recourse than to remain in England until the situation in their homeland could be stabilized. Food was short there, housing in some areas non-existent, and to their credit, to return would be just another body competing for the resources so scarce for their fellow Germans.

This was the situation of the U-boat captain who upon his release in late summer of 1946 and not knowing what to do with his new-found freedom, and still holding in the pocket of his very worn coat the pipe he had taken from the house by the sea so long ago, sought in his heart to visit the place of his capture.

Though he had no other motive, nor any definitive reason to return to the place where his war had ended, he thought it might be an admirable gesture to return the pipe. So armed with only a ration book, a small satchel of food, a very well-stuffed tobacco pouch, and a few other essentials, and aided by the use of an old bicycle and a small sum of money he had procured in exchange for helping an old fisherman overhaul and repair the stuffing box, shaft seals, and bearings in his small yet useful fishing boat (no challenge for the captain of a U-boat whose expertise lay in keeping water out of his vessel), he set off to travel up the western coast of Scotland."

The Old Woman's Tale

By now, I was somewhat intrigued by the lad's story and wanted to hear even more. He quickly continued.

"He had not traveled far, for a bicycle is not a fast mode of transportation, when he encountered an old woman, burdened down with a load of freshly dug peat that she pulled behind her in a very old dilapidated cart whose wooden wheel that ran along the grassy edge of the road wobbled extensively. He started to pass her without speaking, but upon noticing her posture, an unfamiliar sense of empathy bloomed within him.

For as she labored with her load, he could see that the years, yea decades even, of a hard and demanding life had bowed her severely from the middle of her back upward and at that moment was limiting her view of the spectacular countryside to only two or three square meters of the roadbed directly at her well-worn and poorly shod feet.

'May I help you with your load?' he yelled loudly against the noise of the wheels on the rough road in a voice, despite his time in England, that still hung heavy with his native accent.

The old woman stopped and with what appeared to be some great effort, turned toward him, looked up slowly, and after a quick study of the face of this stranger, nodded in agreement. Upon seeing the nod, he dismounted and placed his bicycle gently atop the pile of peat and took her position between the shafts and commenced with the trip.

He had not gone far when he began to hope the destination would not be a long trek, for he began quite quickly to realize he was now using muscles that he had not used in some long time. After about fifteen minutes, he was relieved to hear the old woman speak and upon glancing her way, saw that she was pointing to an opening in the wall next to the road that led gently up a small hill to what looked like an extremely humble croft.

As they approached the house, the old woman spoke and indicated that she wanted the cart pulled around to the back of the house where he saw a small lean-to shed partially stacked with peat. Grateful to have been able to survive the effort, he asked if she wanted it stacked in the shed, and receiving the affirmative nod, he began slowly to stack the contents of the cart in the empty end of the shed, separate from the rest, for the peat she had in the cart did not yet appear quite sufficiently dry for burning.

He had not noticed that she had left him alone to his chore, but upon finishing, he saw her step from the back door of the house with what appeared to be tea and bread. He was not expecting to be rewarded for his labors, but the work had kindled hunger and knowing that his own supply of food was what could be described at best as meager, he gladly accepted the offer.

He leaned against the wobbly wheel to enjoy the meal, when it shifted somewhat under his weight causing him to spill the tea. As he regained his footing, he looked at the wheel, then at her, and then at the slightly darkening sky.

'I can fix that wheel,' he began cautiously. He was rather aggravated with himself for volunteering for such service because the labor in pulling the cart had indeed left him somewhat exhausted.

'In the morning,' the old woman said softly. 'It is getting late and I am tired. Ye can kip in the barn if ye wish or ye can be on your way. There is clean hay there, the rats have all been killed, and my four cats will keep ye quite safe. There is spring water behind the barn, safe to drink.'

Having given her instructions, she collected the tea and cups, turned and stepped into the house and closed the door.

He didn't like the way things had transpired, but she was right; it was getting late, fatigue was very present, and a good night's sleep seemed very desirable and indeed, very necessary.

As he nestled into a bed of hay, as promised, four rather old cats materialized from the darkness at the far end of the barn and surrounded him. He extended his hand, which one by one investigated with a delicate whiff, and having approved of this stranger, three of them withdrew a safe distance and curled up in the hay. The fourth circled him a few times, sniffed curiously at his face, and came to rest not far from his right leg. It was the last thing he saw when sleep descended.

The morning came quickly and to his surprise, he was summoned to the house for a somewhat hearty breakfast of potato pancakes, honey, and to his great delight, coffee.

'Thank you for this breakfast,' he said as he took a seat at her table. 'I wasn't expecting to be treated so well but rest assured, it is appreciated.' Surprisingly, the old woman didn't respond.

After a few morsels of food and a long drink of the coffee, he continued. 'Thanks also for the use of the barn. Although it was a little dusty, I had a very sound sleep.'

'It's not dust,' she suddenly volunteered, ending his assumption that she was forever to remain nearly silent and surprising him that her Scottish was suddenly replaced with more understandable English.

'Pardon?'

'It's not dust. Sit quietly and I will tell ye a tale from long ago. It's a story my grandmother once told me that she had been told by her grandmother and so on all the way back to a gentler time, many, many years ago. The story circulated from generation to generation since its beginning, but only through the female side of the family. Perhaps 'twas told when grandmothers and granddaughters sat quietly churning butter.

Many years ago a little girl, somewhere in the hills of western Scotland, had stumbled upon one of the rarest creatures on planet Earth:

a wounded fairy. How this fairy came to be injured and why at this point in its life it elected to reveal itself to the girl has been lost over the generations, but the tale lives on.

As the girl and the fairy sat in the slowly descending sun of a late summer day, the fairy began to explain things that only her ears had ever heard, for the fairy told her of many of the important things in the life of a fairy.

'Fairies are neither good nor bad,' the fairy began, 'bring neither blessings nor curses, but have but two main purposes in life: to reproduce and to dance.'

Thinking the lass was a tad too young to focus on the reproduction of its ilk, the fairy began to tell her of the wondrous glory of fairy dance.

For it seems that though they love it and it is their second highest priority in life, fairies only dance at night. When a household has retired, and the noise and bustle of the day comes to a silent stillness, tens of thousands of fairies come out to dance. Any surface, on any plane, at any angle, no matter how big, no matter how small, becomes a dancefloor. Throughout the night they dance and dance, skipping, hopping, twirling about, and when the early light of a new day first begins to glow in the sky, the fairies slowly retreat from their joy and return to their places of rest.

'Where do you rest?' the young girl asked.

'Fairies rest inside the heads of idle persons, idiots, fools, imbeciles, dolts, dullards, simpletons, dorks, morons, oafs, dunces, jackasses, lumps, dimwits, dummies, dopes, dumbbells, dumbheads, lamebrains, meatheads, nincompoops, clots, nitwits, numbskulls, goons, ignoramuses, boneheads, dodos, knuckleheads, nimrods, goofs, loons, nits, birdbrains, dipsticks, numskulls, airheads, blockheads, dingbats, dunderheads, lunkheads, and politicians, mostly politicians,' the fairy answered.

'You did ask,' the fairy continued as it observed the confusion written on the face of the young lass.

'Why do you rest in the heads of all of these kinds of people and not in the heads of wise and noble persons?'

'It's because of the emptiness and the silence,' the fairy continued, 'for it is there that we find the space and quiet we need to rejuvenate for another night of dance.'

The fairy went on to explain that they make their entrance into such heads riding the winds of lies, idle chatter, worthless discussions and political rhetoric, mostly political rhetoric. It is there inside that fertile ground of such things that the fairies cover their feet with a strange kind of substance that helps them glide about effortlessly as they dance.

'Why must you cover your feet with this substance every day?' the girl asked.

'Why it must be replaced; for when we dance and skip about, it slowly falls off.'

And so now, you are fully aware that what you found in the barn was not dust but is really nothing more than the stuff of the minds of idle persons, idiots, fools, imbeciles, dolts, dullards, simpletons, dorks, morons, oafs, dunces, jackasses, lumps, dimwits, dummies, dopes, dumbbells, dumbheads, lamebrains, meatheads, nincompoops, clots, nitwits, numbskulls, goons, ignoramuses, boneheads, dodos, knuckleheads, nimrods, goofs, loons, nits, birdbrains, dipsticks, numskulls, airheads, blockheads, dingbats, dunderheads, lunkheads, and politicians, mostly politicians.'

Suffice it to say, the captain was so seriously taken aback by this outpouring of chatter from the old woman that he was speechless. He sat there nearly motionless with the half-empty coffee cup held near his lips when the old woman spoke again.

'Ye mentioned fixing my wagon wheel, did ye not?'

To which the captain nodded in agreement, finished his coffee, and stood to leave.

Having taken nourishment, he commenced with the labor of repairing the wheel of the old cart. To his great relief, the axle and hub were not seriously worn, and with a sizable dollop of grease from the barn, and some significant adjustment of the locking nut, he was able to eliminate nearly all of the wobble. With the task done, he knocked gently on the door, bid his host farewell, gratefully accepted a small portion of meat and bread wrapped in brown paper for which he traded a coupon from his ration book, and with a sincere thanks for the breakfast, mounted his bicycle and headed down the lane to the main road."

The Journey Continues

I was thoroughly convinced the lad was spinning a yarn, but I felt I needed to hear more if only to see where he was going with his tale. I excused myself briefly to secure more tea, and upon my return, the lad continued.

"The greatest portion of the remainder of the day was spent laboring up hills and recuperating on the down side. He reflected on the hospitality he had received from the old woman for such a small amount of labor, and that recollection soon instilled in him the idea that this might be his way of completing his journey, for surely, many of these farms had suffered a loss of men in combat, and from what he could understand, most people were still quite distressed by the war. He felt his shirt pocket, and the presence of his very own ration book gave witness that times were still very hard and a return to normal for even these, the victors in the conflict, might still be some time away.

Eventually fatigue set in as the sun was making its way toward the western horizon. As he searched the countryside for some place where he might pass the night, he noticed what appeared to be an isolated shed only a few meters off the road. Investigation revealed it was apparently abandoned, and after a quick survey for the presence of any undesirable inhabitants, he made a bed of fresh hay and slept the night in peace.

The next morning, upon rising sleepily from his slumber and trying with little success to remove the stiffness that had settled upon him through the night, he was startled to find just outside the opening of the shed, a small, somewhat odd-looking elderly gentleman, he too bent from the waist up, who menacingly pointed his walking stick in his direction and loudly demanded to know who he was and why he was sleeping in the shed.

Assuming the old fellow to be the shed's owner, the captain quickly cleared his throat and spoke.

'My apologies good sir for being here, but I am traveling, and being without sufficient funds to secure proper lodging, I presumed by the somewhat dilapidated condition of this small shed that it was without owner and thus would cause no harm to sleep here for a few hours.'

The captain paused, turned to point into the shed, and continued.

'As you can see, I have taken nothing and have left nothing save the imprint of my body in the hay, and if you'll excuse me, I'll take my bicycle and be on my way.'

The old man held his walking stick up as if hindering the captain's exit and then pointed to the captain's bicycle.

'Aye, since ye have a bicycle, may I assume ye are in possession of the skills necessary to maintain it?'

'I am.'

'Well, well now, seeing that ye have no apparent source of your morning nourishment, I would gladly repay ye with a meal if ye would repair my bicycle. My home is just over that hill and if such a trade is acceptable to ye, please follow me.'

Seeing how it was an acceptable trade, the captain gathered up his belongings, took his bicycle from beside the shed, and followed the old man up the hill to his home.

As they neared the house, the captain could make out what he assumed to be the aroma of sausages and eggs drifting from one of the open windows of the home. The old man led him inside where he saw an old woman, also equally bent from the labors of life, standing before a stove with skillet in hand.

The old man bid him take a seat at the table and he soon returned with a small dented cup and a pot of coffee. He silently set it before the captain and poured the steaming liquid carefully. He then motioned with his free hand for the captain to drink.

The captain sipped the coffee slowly, but with a sense of apprehension. *Suppose after he finished the meal and then would not be able to complete the repairs to the bicycle, what would become of the deal he and the old man had agreed to? Would the old man react in anger?*

He hadn't the time to reason the answer before the old woman placed a plate of sausage and eggs before him, tore a portion of bread from a loaf on the table that had been hidden under a simple white cloth, set it beside the captain's plate, and sat down next to the old man who the captain assumed to be her husband.

'Shouldn't I fix the bicycle before I accept your food?' he asked quietly.

'That won't be necessary,' the old man replied. 'There'll be no problem fixing the bicycle. Now eat, afore it gets cold.'

The food was to say the least, the best he had eaten in a long time. The flavor of the sausage was a delight to his senses and the coffee quite refreshing. Soon the meal was finished and the old man stood and placed his hat on his head.

'We'll be off to the shed, now,' he said to his wife, and looking back at the captain, hesitated only long enough for the captain to know he should follow. The captain stood and thanked the old woman, who continued to remain silent, for the food and stepped out into the light of the rising sun.

The door of the shed screeched loudly and reluctantly as the old man swung it open, and placing a short stick between the cross brace of the door and the ground, propped it open. Inside was a large workbench, a collection of rustic but useable hand tools and a cutout in the wall that the old man propped open to let in the morning light. He pointed to something in the corner of the shed, covered over by a dusty, dark canvas. The captain pulled back the canvas and found the bicycle.

As he wheeled it over to the light, he could see it was in quite bad shape. Both tires were deflated and well deteriorated from age, the chain rusty and hanging loose off the rear sprocket.

'It looks pretty bad,' he said to the owner. 'I think I can fix the chain, but what do we do with the tires? Do you have a tire pump and what do we do if they won't hold air?' The apprehension he felt earlier returned even more strongly.

What will I do if I can't make it rideable? he thought to himself.

As he took inventory of the bench for the right spanner to remove the rear tire, the captain studied its contents carefully. Across the wall behind the bench hung a collection of dusty but usable tools from years gone by. He thought about the number of fairies it had taken to produce so much dust, but quickly returned to the matter at hand.

Out near the end of the bench furthest from the door, was a small stick, somewhat in the form of a tall letter "Y" and about the length of a man's forearm, hanging by a small leather strap on a peg, clearly isolated from the other tools. His curiosity about the stick was kindled, but a noise from near the door reminded him of his purpose for being there. He found the needed tool and set about to remove the wheel and check the condition of the tires."

The Old Man's Tale

Though I could not believe myself, I was fully absorbed into the story and could hardly wait for the lad to move forward, which he did.

"The old man had taken a seat on an old dilapidated bench near the corner and removing an even older pipe from his coat pocket, applied fire to it and after several draws and determining it was lit to his satisfaction, began to speak.

'I'd like to tell ye a story told to me many years ago by an elderly man I met near the fruit vendor of our village market. He told me he was a public servant with no less than 47 years of service. He recounted a story of something he experienced many years ago as a bairn. Being he was a politician, I was inclined to doubt his story, but I will leave it up to you to decide the veracity of the tale, which goes thusly:

'He said that out behind his childhood home lay a parcel of land that was not so easily described. To call it a forest would be to overlook the multitude of brambles, weeds, and underbrush that had accumulated over the decades of the absence of mankind. To call it a thicket would be to ignore the numerous pools of water that were home to reptiles without shoulders, and to call it a swamp would not be right either, for it possessed neither the beauty nor the romance that the image of a swamp at sunset often elicits.

But whatever one would choose to call this patch of wilderness, it was a formidable barrier between himself as a 10-year old laddie and the exploration he felt driven to pursue. For in the days of his youth, he had heard, from those older and therefore wiser than himself, stories of pirate treasure that had been buried along the banks of the creek that flowed into the loch that ran lazily along the other side of this hindrance to his exploration and it frustrated him terribly.

As he mapped out his adventure, he found he had only two options. He could enter the loch downstream near the wee one-lane bridge that traversed the loch's expanse, wade, and or swim the distance to the supposed location of the treasure and commence his search. But that option was replete with danger for at the only accessible point in the water, he and other boys had launched and sunk through most of their years, with rock and BB, many a glass ship. In addition, the slithery occupants of the many pools of water in the wilderness often visited this small stretch of accessible beachhead in search of warming sunlight.

The other option involved trespassing on the land of the somewhat grumpy neighbor to his east. By jumping the fence in the northwest corner of his property and racing at highest speed, a 10-year old laddie could reach a passable section of the fence that crossed the peak of a wee hill that descended easily toward the creek, bypassing the pools of water and most of the brambles and thorns.

So, it came to be, that on one bright, sunny, summer day, the young lad with BB-gun in tow, raced across the neighbors land, jumped the fence and navigated his way to the creek. He explored for most of the day and found many treasures. He found a hidden sandy stretch that reached up gently to a high bank from which pure, clean water flowed out from a small crevice, no doubt one of the many such natural springs that gave the creek its name, Spring Branch.

He found stones, smoothed by the water, sand, and time, relics from earlier explorers probably lost while trying to spear fish for food, several rusty cans, labels long lost to the elements, a few old whiskey bottles, most likely tossed from some passing pedestrian, that had floated lazily along the loch until they beached themselves, but alas, no hidden pirate treasure was to be found.

Despite innumerable visits to the area, the buried treasure escaped him until the passage of time and other interests stole away the young explorer. Many years passed, the treasure long forgotten until a most remarkable event took place. The young lad had grown up, married, and built a home for his wife and family not far from the place where he often jumped the neighbor's fence.

One day, when eyelids are closed and humans are often found in the horizontal position, the man was looking out his back door when he spied, in the light of a particularly bright harvest moon, a badger near the door of his garden shed. Thinking it was about to try to enter his shed, he kept a close eye fixed on the animal. Suddenly as he studied the creature, it stood on its hind legs and looked at the man as if beckoning him to approach.

When he got closer, he could see that the badger was resting wearily upon a staff, a straight piece that he recognized from the branches of the trees near the edge of the wilderness that he as a young lad had often cut for himself to use as arrows for homemade bows.

What shocked him the most was that the badger spoke.

'I am old, weary, frail, and dying,' he began slowly, his voice incredibly weak and raspy, 'but I'm wantin' to tell ye a story. I have lived in the wilderness behind your childhood home for many years, and I and my generations before me have seen many strange things the tales of which have been passed down through the years, decades, aye, centuries even.'

The badger stopped briefly to catch his breath and pull himself more erectly upon his staff before continuing.

'I know ye as a bairn searched for treasure along the loch and the creek that feeds into it and I want to make a deal with ye. I am too old and feeble to hunt, but if ye will bring me food each day, I will lead ye to the treasure, for my ancestors were living here when the pirates first came. We always had watch over the loch and the creek when trappers came and set their traps so we could warn others of their danger. Before too many years, the trappers gave up, but we maintained our vigilance. One late autumn day many, many years ago, a small boat entered the loch and came up the creek, three men and a great box, no doubt heavy with contents for two of the men struggled and cursed as they moved it from the boat to its resting spot.'

'How will ye show me the treasure? Will ye take me there now?' asked the man.

'No, but if ye will bring me food each day, I will lead ye to it. Each day I will be in a different place, each place successively closer to the spot where the treasure is buried.'

'How will I know where ye are? It's a big area and difficult to travel,' the man asked, still not certain he was hearing what he was hearing.

'You shall know where I am for when I hear you in the woods, I will rap three times upon a hollow tree trunk until you find me.'

Having said that, the old badger wandered away into the shadows cast by the trees of the woods.

Bewildered by what he had witnessed, the man returned to his home and argued with his senses. Though he was now a man, the conversation stirred up memories of the old folks' stories of buried treasure, and still possessing a little of the young boy's sense of adventure, decided he would humor the badger, for now, being older and braver, and able to carry weapons for protection against the reptiles without shoulders, he set out the next day in search of the badger.

Not far into the woods on that first day, he heard in the distance tap..., tap..., tap. He followed the sound through bramble and thorn until lo and behold, there resting near the trunk of a somewhat rotten log, lay the old badger. He gently placed an open can of fish at his feet.

'I hope ye like this. I'm not certain what badgers eat,' he said quietly.

The old badger said nothing and the man retreated slowly to the edge of the woods where he had made his entrance.

The next day, he entered the woods again, walked to where he had left the badger the day before, and stood quietly listening to the sounds around him. Suddenly tap..., tap..., tap. As he made his way towards the sound, he was aware that he was indeed getting closer to the creek, and as before, he found the old badger this time resting against the base of a tall tree. He placed the fish near him and eased slowly out of the woods.

And so it continued day after day, one week, then two. On the second day of the third week, the man entered the woods and listened carefully for the tapping. He heard nothing, so he made his way to the area where he had last placed the fish, and there was the old badger, lying peacefully on a soft bed of leaves, eyes closed, the staff at his side. He stooped down to place the fish near him, but as he got close, he could see the old badger had died. As he stood to leave, he noticed, sitting in the center of the fish can from the day before, a single gold coin.

As he stooped to retrieve it, a glint in the corner of his eye caught his attention and upon investigation, found another coin only a few paces away. Again as he stooped to pick up the coin, yet another glitter in the sunlight. And so, as he made his way down the now evident path toward the creek, coin after coin appeared before him until he reached a small hollow under the roots of a massive oak tree. There in the shadows was a box, closed but with a hole neatly chewed through in the corner, gold coins tumbling out upon the ground.

In joy and exuberance, he filled his pockets and returned to the old badger to honor him with a kind and gentle burial, but to his surprise, the badger was no longer there, no sign of him at all save his abandoned staff leaning against the tree. Thinking it would cause no harm, he gathered up the staff and left the woods.'

To this day, the man has never told his story. A portion of his wealth was meagerly spent upon himself and his family. The rest remains this day, somewhere out in the woods, awaiting another 10-year old explorer with imagination."

A Journey to the Woods

Once again, I was fully convinced that the lad was telling tales just for tea and scones, but before I could leave, he continued.

"'Do I know this old politician of whom you speak?' the captain asked quietly as he tightened the last axle nut on the front wheel, thus completing the repairs.

The old man hesitated for what seemed like a long time before answering, and finally, taking a long and deep draw on his pipe, spoke.

'I cannot give ye his name, for if it is noised about, his acquaintances, nay even his dearest friends will surely think him to be mad, but I can say that ye have taken a meal with him, even very recently.'

With that, the old man pulled the pipe slowly to his lips and stared intently at the captain.

'If I were to meet this old politician, would there be something that he would desire of me?'

'Very likely he would desire that ye accompany him into the woods to seek out the treasure that was left behind so many years ago.'

'I see,' said the captain as he pushed the now usable bicycle in the direction of the old man.

'And what would I say to the old politician that would let him know that I knew about his story and that I was willing to help.'

'Ye would say that you have heard a strange tale and that ye have fixed his bicycle.'

The old man stood and reached for the bicycle.

'I have fixed your bicycle,' the Captain said.

'Then we must be off,' the old man said as he pushed past the captain and retrieved the strange stick from its peg. He turned and pushing the bicycle out the door of the shed, started across the yard toward the house.

Back inside the house, the captain noticed two large rucksacks sitting on the table, each bulging at the seams and with a long loaf of bread standing on end protruding from around a half-closed flap at the top. The old man motioned for the captain to pick them up, and headed toward the door.

'We'll be back on the third day,' he said to the old woman, and without other discussion, stepped through the door with the captain close behind.

The two walked nearly silently for several minutes, and upon reaching the edge of the woods, the captain finally broke the silence.

'Three days?'

'Aye, today to travel, tomorrow to seek out the treasure, and the third day to return.'

'Is it a long journey?'

'No, not long, but arduous. It is through hill and dale, but since I am old, and ye are not accustomed to such terrain, we will go slowly and carefully.'

With that, they continued their trek inward across the land, generally moving in a northeasterly direction until just as the shadows were stretching to their limit, they reached the bank of a small creek.

'We'll stop here for the night. The water is drinkable and we can build a small fire here near these trees,' the old man said as he took a seat on the ground and released a very weary sigh.

After a brief rest, he regained his breath and continued.

'In the rucksacks are groundsheets, sufficiently suitable for this time of year. With a small fire, we will be quite comfortable for the evening.'

Taking the hint, the captain gathered up a supply of small limbs and branches and started a small fire between two large overhanging trees.

Darkness fell swiftly there in the woods and soon, after some dried beef and a generous portion of the loaf, the two men, weary from the trek, drifted effortlessly off to sleep."

The Strange Encounter

Unexpectedly, I had become hooked by what he was telling me, and seeing my fascination, the lad continued with renewed enthusiasm.

"Morning came later than usual in the woods, for to the east, the canopy of the trees and a rather steep deeply wooded hill blocked the light from the rising sun so much that it was nearly mid-morning before they were fully awake and ready to go.

Having finished a small morsel of bread with honey and just as they had packed the groundsheets into the rucksacks, somewhere from deeper in the woods a voice called out to them.

'Would ye be looking for me?' it asked in a most unusual, almost musical tone.

Thinking he was somehow still half asleep and in some odd dream state, the captain looked at the old man who turned in the general direction of the sound, peering deeply into the shadows in search of the source of this strange voice.

'I say again, are ye looking for me?'

'Perhaps,' said the old man as he moved slowly and cautiously toward the voice.

'I seek the keeper of the treasure. Would ye be a descendent of the one I met so many years ago?'

'Perhaps,' said the still unseen person of the voice. 'What proof do I have that ye are the one spoken of by my ancestors?'

The old man reached into his rucksack and retrieved the small stick that had been hanging in the shed.

'I offer this as proof,' said the old man as he extended the stick in the direction of the voice. 'It was the staff of he who first showed me the gold.'

A brief moment of silence was followed by some rustling in the underbrush and the emergence of a small shadowy figure from behind a rather large tree.

'Come forward,' said the figure, still mostly unrecognizable from the shadows that covered the forest floor.

The old man advanced until he reached a small patch of the woods where the sun was brightly illuminating the ground. He held the stick at arm's length and remained motionless.

The dark figure finally emerged from the protection of the shadows and into the light to reveal a rather large badger.

The captain was so taken aback that he nearly collapsed to the ground.

'You there,' shouted the badger, 'Do ye think it so strange that I can talk?'

The captain stuttered briefly, but the words remained unformed in his brain and only an unintelligible utterance that remained mostly stuck in his throat could be heard.

'Why are ye surprised so? Does not thine own Holy Scriptures speak of such things? Did not your own Creator tell thee that if humans hold their praise that even the rocks would cry out? What about Balaam's donkey, did it not rebuke its master after he had struck it?'

After composing himself, the badger continued. 'Then why think ye that it so strange that I should speak to you?'

The captain slowly regained his composure and the old man began to speak.

'I do not seek all of the treasure, but only a small portion for my descendants. Times are hard now and just a few coins would suffice. As for my friend here, I know not what he would desire, perhaps only a small token as a reminder that what has happened here is indeed real.'

'And what is to our advantage if I lead ye to the treasure? Though we have no real value in the gold of humans, we do know it to be of tremendous value to you and your ilk.'

The badger paused briefly and then continued. 'I know ye to be a man of integrity for if you had revealed the presence of this treasure to others, our woods would be overrun with those seeking the gold, and our habitat would have been destroyed many years ago.'

The badger thought for a minute and then continued, 'So, I make you this agreement. Swear to me that ye will take only what ye need of the treasure and keep your silence until your death, and I will lead ye to where we have stored the chest.'

'What about the captain here?' asked the old man. 'I have not known him long and cannot vouch for his silence in the matter and I have brought him along only because I am too feeble to make the trek alone.'

The badger paused to consider what the old man had said then responded slowly. 'Then either he must die here and now, or ye must take all of the treasure unto yourself and relieve us of its burden, for we want no longer to live in fear of man's search for the treasure as it would be such an unwelcomed intrusion into our peaceful world.'

The old man thought for a moment and replied. 'I can neither kill this one nor take all of the treasure unto myself. I have no real need for all of it, and so much treasure would be as big a burden unto me as it is for you.'

The old man and the badger fell silent for what seemed like a very long time when finally the badger spoke.

'Remain here in this location while I go and speak to my elders concerning this matter. I will return with a solution before the sun has set.' With that, he slipped quietly away and out of sight.

The old man and the captain sat motionless and in total solitude for a very long time. Eventually the captain composed himself and spoke.

'I'm completely taken aback by this,' he said, quickly realizing his voice was quivering and breathing seemed difficult. 'Surely what has just happened here is not real and is the result of some kind of weariness of the soul or some spell found in the thickness of these woods.'

'No, it's very much real,' the old man replied. 'So real, that if it were not real, we would not be in such a state of uncertainty.'

The remainder of the afternoon passed so very slowly, each hour bringing with it the thought that the badger would not return and that the quest for the treasure would evaporate with the going down of the sun.

The captain eventually collected his thoughts and spoke. 'Would it be such a loss if the badger did not return? When I slept in your shed, I had no thought of awakening to a tale of badgers and gold, nor had I any desire for such a thing. Should no more of this come to pass, have we not had an adventure of such note that we could not be content with that alone?'

'For ye and for me, aye it is enough, the old man said, 'but what if we should desire to share this story with our posterity, for an untold story soon loses its value. What would be our proof of such a tale? Would such a story leave them with only the legacy of a madman?'

'This is true,' mumbled the captain who soon fell back into his silence and his thoughts.

Not long after, a rustling in the woods brought the men out of their thoughts and back into the presence of the badger.

'I have consulted with my elders and we have come to this undisputable agreement. Ye must take all of the treasure unto yourselves, swear to complete silence in the matter of where it was located, and each year until your death, as a token of your agreement, you must present to your God, a small offering in appreciation of your new fortune. Should ye pass this story down to your descendants, ye must not reveal the location of these woods, but if demanded of you, speak of it no more than only as somewhere in western Scotland. Do we have an agreement?'

The two men looked at one another and after a few seconds, nodded in agreement.

'We agree to these terms,' said the old man.

With that, the badger led them over a small hill to a place along the bank of the creek and to a small crevice under a large tree. There, deep within the darkness was a large chest, covered over by years of solitude.

The two men quickly rid the chest of its contents, stuffed the large leather sacks of coins into their rucksacks, and turned to thank the badger for his troubles. The woods were still and quiet; no one was to be seen.

Slowly the two men made their way back to where they had spent the night, the short journey now more burdensome from the weight of their newfound treasure, and settled down for a night's sleep before heading back to the old man's croft.

Sleep did not come easily for them, for not only did their minds run amuck with the idea of their newfound wealth, but also a certain worry about being in possession of such a treasure stole away their ability to rest. The fears of robbery turned every sound in the moonlit woods into thieves and every shadow into muggers creeping about with murderous intentions. Moreover, on top of everything else, the rucksacks, which had served them well as pillows the night before, now were hard, lumpy, and cold from the coins.

So in the morning of the third day, the two men began the journey homeward. The burden of the weight of the coins so slowed them that it was well after dark before the familiar sight of the old man's croft came into view.

Their conversation had been sparse throughout the day, and upon approaching the house, the old man inquired of the captain his intentions.

'I suppose if it is permissible, I'd like to sleep in the old shed down by the road and be on my way in the morning.'

'Aye,' the old man replied. 'That is permissible. I'll get you a morsel of bread and some meat from the kitchen and bid you good night and goodbye. Speak no more of me or these events for as long as you live.'

Having accepted the food, and extending a well-meaning thank you for the hospitality, the food, and the adventure, the two parted company.

Again, sleep eluded the captain, and after a restless night, he soon mounted his bicycle and continued his journey toward the place of his capture."

More Travel, More Encounters

Finally, the absurdity of such a story snapped me out of my fascination and I decided it was time to abandon this lad, but he refused to stop talking.

"Riding up the hills was now even more burdensome for the captain. Not only did the added weight of the treasure make it more difficult, but also three days of walking the hills and sleeping in the outdoors had left his legs most unusable for biking. He considered taking a few days in a boarding house, but dismissed it as unacceptable, again because of fears about protecting the gold. Soon he began to realize the treasure was not a treasure at all, but in all reality a very serious issue. He had to devise a plan to deal with his newfound wealth to relieve him of its burden.

Perhaps there is no better place to think than on a bicycle on a quiet road in the vast expanse of western Scotland. He reflected on those who had originally hidden the treasure, why they thought they needed to hide it, why they picked that particular location, and what might have been their plans for when to return for it. Then his thoughts turned to why they had not returned for it. Had they been caught, killed, or perhaps lost at sea as they searched for even more treasure?

Then his thoughts turned to how he might benefit from this newfound wealth. How would he spend it? How would he convert it to local currency, for surely there must be some regulations concerning found treasure, especially if it were historically noteworthy, since to his recollection, he was certain the gold coins were Spanish doubloons.

To convert one of the doubloons to spendable money would certainly raise a lot of questions and probably even the ire of the law.

Before too many miles had passed, the captain was now quite full of remorse for accepting any of the coins. Perhaps if he had asked the old man how he was planning to redeem his coins, he might now have a better appreciation for this treasure.

The morning gradually turned to afternoon and soon the captain was thinking about when and where to find a place of rest. His own personal rations and the food given him by the old man had been consumed, and his need for rest grew stronger with each hill. Eventually it became necessary to stop at the peak of each hill to catch his breath and rest.

So atop an unusually tall hill, he pulled the bicycle into the grass and sat slowly against the cool, stone wall, his legs begging for relief from the pain. As he rubbed them to increase the circulation, he surveyed his surroundings, taking no delight in what he saw for nowhere in the view from that particular hill could he see barn, shed or house wherein he might bed down.

More regret began to set in as he considered the contrast of his two endeavors. The pipe that was the impetus of his journey was nearly worthless and the gold coins in the sack near his side nearly priceless. Yet the worthless pipe brought him great comfort as he packed the tobacco and lit it, and the priceless gold brought him only anguish and worry.

'What a contrast!' he exclaimed out loud.

'What is it that is such a contrast?' asked a voice from behind the wall.

Startled, he leaped to his feet and steadied himself on wobbly legs as he leaned over the wall to find the owner of the voice. Lying in the grass with a pipe of his own was yet another weary old man, very short in stature.

'Ah,' continued the man after seeing the captain's pipe dangling loosely from his mouth. 'Would ye have a wee bit of tobacco for me pipe?'

Without speaking, the captain extended his tobacco pouch which the man took and applied a small portion to his bowl.

'Have you a light?'

Without thinking, the captain searched his pockets and extended his lighter to the old man. Throughout his days as a POW, he had tried without much success to erase the insignia on the side of the lighter and to his dismay, the old man noticed it and studied it briefly in the bright sunlight before returning it.

'Ah, I know who you are,' he said in a voice that triggered a strange feeling in the pit of the captain's stomach. 'What brings ye out this far away from the Castle?'

'Sightseeing mostly,' the captain replied, trying desperately hard to minimize the exchange of information. 'I was captured not too many miles up the coast and thought I would return and pay my respects to the lady who briefly held us prisoner.'

'I've heard tales of that,' the old man mused as he drew heavily on the pipe. 'For a long time, the Navy had assumed ye had gone down with your boat. It wasn't until your stay at the Castle that the records caught up with reality and word made it back here.'

'It was a difficult time for all of us,' the captain replied, trying hard not to say anything that might trigger an unacceptable response from the old man.

'Ah, aye, but more difficult for some than for others. There are many here who still hold strong feelings of anger about the war, especially those who lost their menfolk to the Wolfpacks. Perhaps it is not wise of you to travel here, especially alone. Do ye not fear for your life?'

'So far,' responded the captain, 'I have found nothing more threatening than indifference. Some have even extended to me their table and hospitality in exchange for a bit of labor.'

'Ah aye, and I guess that's how it should be seeing the world is in such a state. Well, if you'll allow me a wee bit more from your pouch, I'll be on my way for I too am a wayfaring stranger, tossed about by the indifference of this old world.'

Again, the captain extended his pouch; the old man stuffed his pipe again and stood to be on his way.

'Oh, by the way, if you go about three more miles, there is a farm just past the next bridge that might be open to an exchange of labor for a warm spot of hay. Tell them Wee Laddie Will sent you.'

Without further words, the two parted company and with it, a sense of relief came over the captain. Not since his release had he been challenged about his role in the war, and to his great satisfaction, he felt good about how he had handled himself with this stranger."

Opposing Sides Meet

I had begun to wonder just how the captain might respond if he should stumble upon someone who had indeed suffered the loss of a loved one, when the lad resumed his tale.

"The miles to the farm seemed to pass more easily and soon he was turning off the road and peddling up the hill to the croft. At some distance from the house, a dog began to bark, and shortly thereafter, the door swung open revealing a woman about his own age, wiping her hands on the bottom of her rather large apron.

He spoke as soon as he got within earshot of the woman. 'Hello, Wee Laddie Will said you might have a dry place to sleep in exchange for some labor. Is that true?'

'Oh, he did, did he?' she responded as she held her place in the doorway and leaned against the frame. 'What kind of work can you do?'

'Mostly anything, but I'm more useful at things mechanical.'

'Well other than the daily farm chores, I have no other work. If ye would like to stay in the barn there, in the morning ye can assist with the chores and be on your way. There is some soup and fresh bread here if ye are hungry. You can wash up out by the barn.'

It was a welcome invitation and soon he was seated at a rather large wooden table in her kitchen.

'Your speech betrays you; are you German?' she asked without hesitation as she drew near and handed him the bowl of soup and a large piece of the fresh loaf.

'Yes, I was a prisoner of war at the Castle from 1944 until just recently.'

'Where did you learn your English?'

'I attended school in England many years before the war. Strange as it sounds, I majored in English and English literature.'

She stood silently for a brief moment and studied his face as he dipped a morsel of bread in the soup.

'Did ye embrace the Nazi mindset?'

The captain swallowed hard and answered cautiously. 'Not really. I swore allegiance to the fatherland and to the crew of the boat I captained, but the ideals of the Führer were foreign to me, maybe if I be truthful, perhaps even somewhat frightening. Perhaps that was the reason I wasn't a very good captain as it turned out, only one victory to my credit and my career ended just outside Loch Ewe.'

The woman returned to the sink and began to tidy the dishes she had used to make the soup.

'I've heard that story many times from some friends up near there,' she said as she turned her head slightly to speak over her shoulder. 'Seems there was some woman who captured the whole crew singlehandedly.'

'Well, not exactly, there were only three of us. All the rest of my crew was taken prisoner by the Navy.'

After a short pause, he clumsily inquired of her life at the farm. 'Are you running this farm all alone?'

She stopped what she was doing, turned, and looked at him with a very stern expression.

'I am not alone. I have a friend who stays in my waistband that I can call upon in an instant. In fact, it wasn't but a few hours ago that I sent your Wee Laddie Will skipping across the yard with a few well-placed bursts at his feet. So don't be getting any ideas about the needs of a woman on her own.'

'I meant neither harm nor threat!' the captain explained as he raised his hands in the surrender position and sat back from the table. 'I'm grateful for the meal and the use of the barn and come morning I'll be on my way unless you wish me to stay and help with the chores.'

'There'll be some chores in the morning. I'll be out with a bit of breakfast shortly after that noisy, big-mouthed rooster starts up, so be ready and alert.'

Finishing the soup and taking the last of the bread with him, the captain bid her good evening and retired to the barn. With a content stomach, sleep came easily for him.

As promised, the rooster started just as the sun broke the horizon. Unfortunately for the captain, the noisy beast had roosted almost directly overhead in the barn and very nearly bombed him with a morning deposit that fell at the first crow. Shortly after, the woman appeared with bread and sausage, and before long, the chores were completed.

'It does go faster with help,' she admitted when they had completed the last chore. 'Wash up and come in the house for a cup of coffee and then you can be on your way.'

The captain did as requested, but before leaving the barn, he quietly opened the large leather sack and slipped two of the coins into his jacket pocket.

Soon he was seated at the table with cup in hand. The woman was working near the stove when he broke the silence.

'So how is it that you are alone? Forgive me if this is disrespectful, but you are an attractive woman and it seems unusual to me that there is not a husband here.'

Without turning, she replied. 'Oh, I had one, a really good one in fact, but he died in North Africa. Your lot down there sent a bunch of shells into where he was sleeping and buried him in multiple pieces right on the spot.'

In a hushed tone, the captain responded slowly and thoughtfully, 'I'm so sorry.'

He hesitated while he collected his thoughts and then continued. 'At the outset, we all thought this war was an honorable thing, but it didn't take very long for some of us to see that it had no possibility of a good outcome, but we were obligated to see it through to the end.'

'Those were nearly the exact words from my husband in the last letter I received from him. He too had grown weary of killing Germans and though he hated it and what it was doing to him, he felt he needed to see it to a conclusion.'

Another moment of silence fell on them until the captain breached yet another personal question.

'What do you intend to do? Will you keep the farm?'

'I'll keep it as long as I can. I have no other source of income or any other place to call home. I have friends and some relatives in the area that I can call on if needed.'

She hesitated before continuing and in a very soft voice said, 'Perhaps love will visit me again although the prospects are few.'

'Would you come back to the table?' the captain asked quietly.

The woman came and sat silently, one hand on the table, the other resting lightly on the waistband of her skirt.

'I have something I want to give you, but you must not ask any questions nor tell anyone where you got it. Can you agree to that?'

'Aye, but be careful,' she responded as she deliberately patted her hand noisily against her waistband.

Fully understanding what she meant, the captain carefully reached into his jacket pocket, pulled out the coins, and slid them slowly across the table to within her reach.

She cautiously picked them up and studied them carefully.

'Do you have a way to exchange them for your currency?' he asked.

'I'm not sure. These appear to be rare Spanish Doubloons, probably worth more than their actual gold value, but I do know someone who is a coin collector who rarely asks questions and is quite honest in his valuation.'

'Well, I hope you can redeem them. If asked, just tell them a packrat must have brought them into your barn or you found them washed ashore near here.'

'Where did you get them?' she demanded with suspicion. 'Did you steal them?'

'I'm sworn to secrecy, but I came by them honestly; I didn't steal them. You might say they were given to me, and I in turn am giving them to you.'

'But why to me?' she asked again, in a tone that was somewhat less demanding.

'The war produced no good result, only pain, sadness, death, and destruction. I too have suffered loss. My family was killed and my home destroyed by the invading Russian army. A simple gold coin or two cannot replace your husband, but they might somehow help reduce your struggles and hopefully provide some measure of hope that things will get better.'

With that said, the conversation ended, the woman stood from the table and returned to her kitchen, packed a small portion of ham and bread in some brown paper and handed it to the captain who then stepped out into the warmth of the midday sun. As he pedaled away, she shouted 'thank you' from the door and waved. The captain was grateful he heard no gunshots."

Getting Closer to the Croft

By this time, I was beginning to wonder if the lad's story was ever going to have a conclusion, but not knowing how to hurry him along, I remained silent, and he continued.

"Out on the road again, the captain thought about the recent exchanges of labor for food and a place to sleep and it occurred to him that had he purchased the food and lodging with the gold coins he had given away, he certainly didn't get a fair exchange, for surely the coins would have commanded at least a month of fine dining and exquisite lodgings in the finest establishments. But all the same, it felt good that he had been able to help someone in need.

Finally, the captain was getting close to his destination. He was certain that he was but a couple of days away from reaching the place where he and his two crewmen had come ashore, but one, maybe two nights separated him from his goal. He realized he had not thought things through very well for once he returned the pipe to the old woman, he really would have no place to go. The thought suddenly erupted upon him that he was indeed homeless.

Though he didn't enjoy being a prisoner of war, at least there in the Castle he had a comfortable place with acceptable meals that was his every night. Now, with no predictable outlook, he felt strangely aware of just how much the war had cost him and it troubled him deeply. His wife and daughter dead, his home destroyed by the Russian Army, his life totally upended by the whimsical desires of, yes, he could finally admit it to himself, a madman, all overwhelming him to the point of desperation. He wondered if it all might not make of him too, a madman.

He soon arrived at the outskirts of a small village and was reminded of his hunger. He still had most of the money he had earned from repairing the fishing boat, so he decided it might be time to partake of a real meal and perhaps refill his tobacco pouch. He was grateful that the pub appeared to be mostly empty, but at the same time, he thought there might have been some advantages if it were crowded, for he could very likely go unnoticed in a crowd.

Once inside he ordered a pub meal, which he found to be quite enjoyable. He was certain his attention to his belongings was observed by several of those in attendance, which left him feeling quite uncomfortable.

How do I make my exit without attracting attention, and what do I do if I am followed? he thought to himself. The awareness of the treasure he held in his sack once more weighed him down with regret. If only he had not agreed to the deal proffered by the badger, he felt he could be quite at ease.

He now understood why the badgers so easily gave up the treasure. Certainly the weight of the knowledge of such a treasure for so many years had been a burden to them, but as he pondered it, he realized just what an unreasonable idea it was to even think he had been talking and dealing with an animal. Surely, this too would eventually drive him insane if he continued to wrestle with it.

Eventually the pub owner approached him.

'You look troubled my friend. Can I get ye a drink?'

'Yes, I think I'll have a small brandy, please sir, and a bottle to take with me to chase the night's chill.'

'Coming right up.'

The brandy arrived very quickly and with it, the questions began: *Who are you? Where are you going? What is your purpose here?*

And finally the big one. *Do you have some place to stay?*

With the answer to the negative, the pub owner invited him, with no uncertainty, to leave. So, with rucksack in hand, the captain slipped quietly out into the evening and quickly rode away into the approaching darkness.

After a few miles, the darkness was such that he could barely see the road. Upon stopping, he could hear what he thought was the sea, so he dismounted the bike and walked it carefully in the direction of the sound. As the sound grew louder, he could at times pick up the scent of the water and finally he drew near the shore and could see the open expanse. Oh, the memories it brought back of all those years out on the open water and the pain of realizing that yet another of life's simple joys had been taken from him soon overwhelmed him.

Weariness set in quickly, aided by the sound of the waves crashing against the rocks on the shore and soon it was impossible to ignore the need for sleep. He wrapped himself in his groundsheet, curled up behind a large rock safely out of reach of the tide and drifted off to sleep."

Finally There

Suddenly, without a word, the lad left the table and disappeared into the loo. He soon returned and without missing a beat, resumed his story.

"Morning brought with it an awareness that this journey might have been a mistake for the captain. The difficult days of riding, the trials of sleeping rough, and a diet that to say the least was poor, were beginning to take their toll, for it was becoming more difficult to regain the strength to pedal so many miles.

But with no other option, he soon walked the bike back to the road and resumed his northerly direction. Mile after mile soon passed until a slow sensation of familiarity began to encroach upon him. He noticed a road sign that showed him to be but a few miles south of his destination. He continued to pedal, more slowly now as he studied the many crofts and the small houses that lay at the end of each of the paths leading away from the road.

Soon he spotted what he was certain was a familiar house. Looking back toward the sea, he could see clearly the area where they had beached their raft that stormy night those years ago. Oddly, nothing seemed to have changed for even the rocks at the water's edge looked so familiar.

Mustering up his courage, he approached the large wooden door and knocked gently. He paused briefly and then knocked again, this time with more effort. Soon the handle turned and he found himself once again facing the double barrels of the 12 bore, a sight that had never left his memory since that stormy night.

'Please madam, if you could, can you remember me?'

The barrels of the 12 bore slowly descended and my great-great grandmother moved closer and stared directly into his face.

'Do ye have my pipe?' she asked sternly.

'Yes, madam, I do,' he responded as he reached into his jacket pocket to retrieve the pipe and then pulled his tobacco pouch from the rucksack, 'and a bit of tobacco to replace that which I used.'

'Well, ye may as well come in,' she said as she placed the gun down in the corner near the door. 'Where did ye come from and how did ye get here?' she asked. 'Have ye been set free or did ye escape?'

'Yes, Madam, I was released from the Castle in September last year and after wandering about for a while, I bought a bicycle and pedaled my way up here.'

'And why have ye come?'

'To return your pipe, of course. I thought it the proper thing to do, since it was I who took it.'

'Well, I have no need for it. Ye may as well keep it. I suppose you'll be wanting some tea too?'

'Well, it would be very much welcomed, thank you.'

'Ye may as well take a seat. Come into the kitchen so I can keep an eye on ye. The last thing I want is for ye to steal any more of my pipes.'

The captain humored my great-great grandmother for he knew she must have been kidding. Her general lack of true animosity hinted to him that perhaps the war had been kinder to her than most.

'I hate to intrude where it may be painful, but have your loved ones returned safely from the war?' he asked as he took a seat at her table.

'My two sons are safe. One has returned to me and is living farther down the coast, and the other is soon to return. He stayed in Germany after the war as part of the occupational forces and is scheduled to return a bit later this year. The silly fool went and married one of you lot and is bringing her and her mother here to live. Times are tough over there and he is still war weary, even yet so long after the combat has ended.'

'I must say I am surprised what with so many available women here in your own country, but I think you will find the girl will please you as most German women are very devoted to their husbands. Perhaps if I am around, I might help her acclimate to life here in Scotland. I have certainly found most of you to be gentle and kind people.'

'So, what are your plans?' my great-great grandmother asked as she placed a cup on the table and slowly poured the tea.

'I have no plans,' he continued as he pulled the brandy from his rucksack and placed the bottle gently on the table, 'other than to replace the brandy we consumed. Other than that, I am at a total loss as to what to do. My family have all been killed, my beloved house destroyed, and the Russians now control my part of Berlin. I am indeed a man without a country. I have considered finding a way to get to America, but that seems just as difficult as finding a new life here. Truth be told, I was better off in the POW camp.'

With nothing more to say, the captain directed his attention to the tea placed before him.

'Well, perhaps we can work something out. My son who is returning soon from Germany has asked that I find a suitable spot for him to build. He wants to stay in the RAF and has secured a position not far from Loch Ewe. Perhaps you might be able to help him build his house.'

She paused briefly then added. 'There is also a lot of demand for help from the owners of the fishing boats. If ye can find work there, and ye can help my son, I'll agree to let you stay here if ye can adjust to staying out in the barn.'

The captain readily agreed, but unexpectedly in just a few days, he was pleasantly surprised to learn that one of the close neighbors of my great-great grandmother had a small house nearby that she was willing to let to anyone who would help her with some renovations to her main house, an agreement that was most desirable to the captain as he now had a place that he could call home for a while.

Sleeping in barns and sheds had become very old and somewhat painful for him as the years were gradually taking their toll on him. So with great gratitude he took up residence not far from my great-great grandmother and became a resident handyman, mechanic to the fishing boats, and supervisor of construction on the future home of the old woman's son."

Unexpected Surprise

Surely, I assumed, the story had finally reached its conclusion. I started to slide my chair away from the table in preparation to leave, but as before, the lad continued to relate his tale.

"Time passed quickly and at the first sign of autumn of 1947, the son returned with his new wife and her mother. Not many days later, the three came out to visit the site of their new home where the captain was inside finishing a few details concerning the operation of one of the windows on the front of the house. There seemed to be some misalignment of the locking mechanism and as he struggled with it, he glanced up to see the three approaching. He had heard that they had returned, but until now had not met them.

As they drew closer, a strange and somewhat frightening sensation began to grow in his chest. There was something familiar about the appearance of the two women. Soon they were clearly visible and the reality hit the captain like a blow to his chest, opening the floodgates of his eyes. For there, walking up the lane to the house were none other than his wife and daughter who he had been told had died in the war. No words can accurately describe the next few moments in the captain's life, but suffice it to say, such degree of happiness had rarely been observed in the post-war years as took place that day.

The following years passed in much joy and contentment and the child the captain's daughter carried in her womb that day had grown into a brilliant lad who held some great fascination for the ships at sea and would spend countless hours in the attic of his home staring through the window at the lights of the ships as far out to the horizon as he could see. Realizing the lad's interest was not a fleeting fancy but a sincere interest in the sea and the ships that sailed her, the captain sought out and purchased a navy surplus radio receiver from a discrete individual who gladly accepted a strange gold coin in exchange.

So over the weeks, through hours of listening, the captain taught the young lad the radio code, and each evening as the sun set and the lights of ships on the water became visible, the two would tune the shipping frequencies and listen to the ships calling the harbor masters and exchanging radio messages across the seas."

The Truth Comes Out

Unexpectedly, the lad, who had stared out the window for most of his story, sat back quietly for a few seconds and then glanced up at me with a strange look in his eyes and said, "Sir, I must confess to you that some of what I have told you is not true."

Ah, I thought to myself. *I knew this was the imaginations of a young boy mixed with a touch of deceptive spirit thinking that he could amuse himself by wasting the time of an adult.*

"I thought so," I replied. "Have you ever considered becoming a writer of fiction?" I asked somewhat sarcastically. "You seem to have quite the imagination."

He looked at me with all sincerity in his eyes and said, "No sir, the story is true, every detail, for from the captain on down through history, my ancestors have all been meticulous at keeping journals. I have read them countless times, so much so that every detail is committed to memory."

He paused briefly and continued.

"I lied about visiting relatives in the south of England. In fact, I have just returned this morning from the Spanish Embassy in London where I surrendered the sack of gold doubloons the captain found those many years ago."

"And how do I know this to be true?" I asked, this time with a clearly evident tone of disbelief and sarcasm.

The lad looked at me for what seemed like an eternity, obviously in disbelief of my unbelief, slowly reclined somewhat in his chair, reached into the pocket of his trousers, and withdrew a small coin that he placed on the table directly at my fingertips.

From his backpack, he pulled a cardboard tube that he also placed on the table and sliding it slowly in my direction said simply, "Open and read it."

From inside the tube I withdrew a stiff piece of parchment paper that I unrolled and flattened against the table. It was a certificate of ownership written in both English and Spanish declaring that the holder of this certificate was the clear and legal owner of one (1) Spanish Seville Gold 8 Escudos Doubloon, dated 1810.

He then pulled from his shirt pocket a bank draft from a prominent London bank for the incredible amount of forty-five thousand pounds sterling.

"It's a gift from the Spanish embassy, a form of finder's fee or reward I guess," he said somewhat sadly as he held the check and studied the writing.

I picked up on the tone of his voice and asked him why he would be sad, for it seemed such money and the certificate would have many a young lad rejoicing.

"For another cup of tea and one more scone, I'll finish the story."

I thought *here we go again*, but I agreed, and when I returned with the tea and scone, he continued.

"That sack of gold has been handed down from generation to generation, and with it came its burden, always a burden. It was an immense treasure all those years that we McGintys have held but didn't own; a fortune that we could not spend; a burden that we could only pass down to the next generation. In every generation for those who knew the secret of the source of the treasure, that sack of gold became a millstone around our necks. For some, it nearly drove them mad, for others it so occupied their thinking that they became nearly useless to their families."

He paused to take a bite from the scone and a sip of the tea and continued.

"I could see it was beginning to take its toll on my own father, for there was a sense of lunacy creeping upon him. So, last night I stole the sack from its hiding place to end this burden of so many years."

He paused briefly and with a decidedly more somber tone in his voice said, "I must now face my father and tell him what I have done, for neither did I want to see this madness come upon him, nor, since I was next in line to hold the treasure, pass the burden to my own children should that day come to be."

He stopped and looked at me for my response. To say the least, I was quite without words at the wisdom and courage of this young lad.

"I'm sorry I didn't believe your story," I started. "You must admit that it seemed hard to fathom. Nevertheless, I trust you have indeed done the right thing. Perhaps the reward money will soften your father's response?"

My thoughts suddenly changed and I continued my questioning, "What if he has arisen this morning and found the gold missing. Wouldn't he also realize that you too are gone?"

"That is part of the dilemma," the young lad said. "You must understand that my father has no other option but anger. He cannot call the authorities to report his gold as stolen, and to report me as missing would prompt a lot of questions whose answers would open a box that cannot be closed."

The conversation fell silent and soon thereafter, we could hear the horn of an approaching train. The stationmaster announced the destination of the train and the lad stood to leave.

"I wish you well," I said as he walked to the door.

He stopped, turned to me, returned to the table, and placed the doubloon and its certificate on the table.

"Take this," he said sternly, "for it carries a burden of its own, the sole evidence of a story that others will want to hear, that will open a link to the past that must now be forever forgotten. If I am to end the burden of the badgers' gold, it must end completely; it must end now."

He glanced at me briefly, then turned, and with single-minded determination left the tea room and boarded the train.

The last I saw of the lad, he was seated in the train at a window, facing forward, and staring into what would most certainly be a somewhat stormy day.

Epilog

But alas, as is common with all such fragments of history, the story really doesn't end there. A year later while on a business trip, I paid a visit to the Spanish Embassy in London, and feigning only a slight interest in a bit of gossip I had heard, I inquired of the gold. They indicated the gold had eventually been returned to Spain, and was placed on exhibit for a while at a prestigious museum in Madrid with only a simple notation that the treasure had been discovered buried somewhere in western Scotland. No other details were provided other than the dates of the various coins and their current value which some estimates placed at 4.5 million pounds sterling.

Some years later I checked up on Billy McGinty. He had become a professor of Scottish history at a prominent university in northern Scotland, specializing in folklore tales, their origins, and their historical significance. He has published several in-depth volumes on the subject, some that tell of fairies, some of the monsters of the deep waters, but none that mention badgers.

Don't miss out!

Visit the website below and you can sign up to receive emails whenever Wiley Traylor publishes a new book. There's no charge and no obligation.

https://books2read.com/r/B-A-SJAS-KNFWB

Connecting independent readers to independent writers.

Also by Wiley Traylor

The Strange Tale of Billy McGinty
The Porches of 101 North Pine Street
Isaiah's Farm
We Had a Window Fan
The Ordinary Life of Anderson Lane

About the Author

Wiley Traylor is an amateur writer who writes for fun. Born a long time ago in a small town in Louisiana, he now abides in Tennessee where he spends his retirement thinking about and writing stories of adventure with an element of mystery and developing characters whom he would like to meet one day.

www.ingramcontent.com/pod-product-compliance
Lightning Source LLC
Chambersburg PA
CBHW020933160726
47993CB00007B/2758